SWARM OF BEES
LEMONY SNICKET
Art by Rilla Alexander

ANDERSEN PRESS

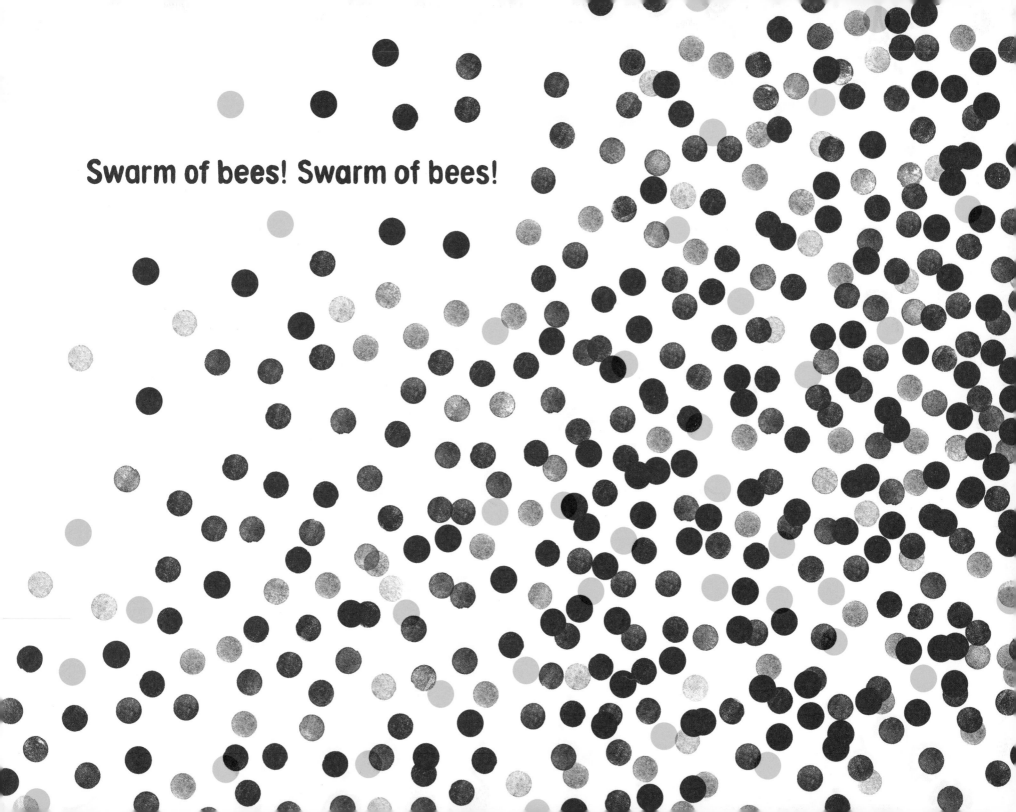

Swarm of bees! Swarm of bees!

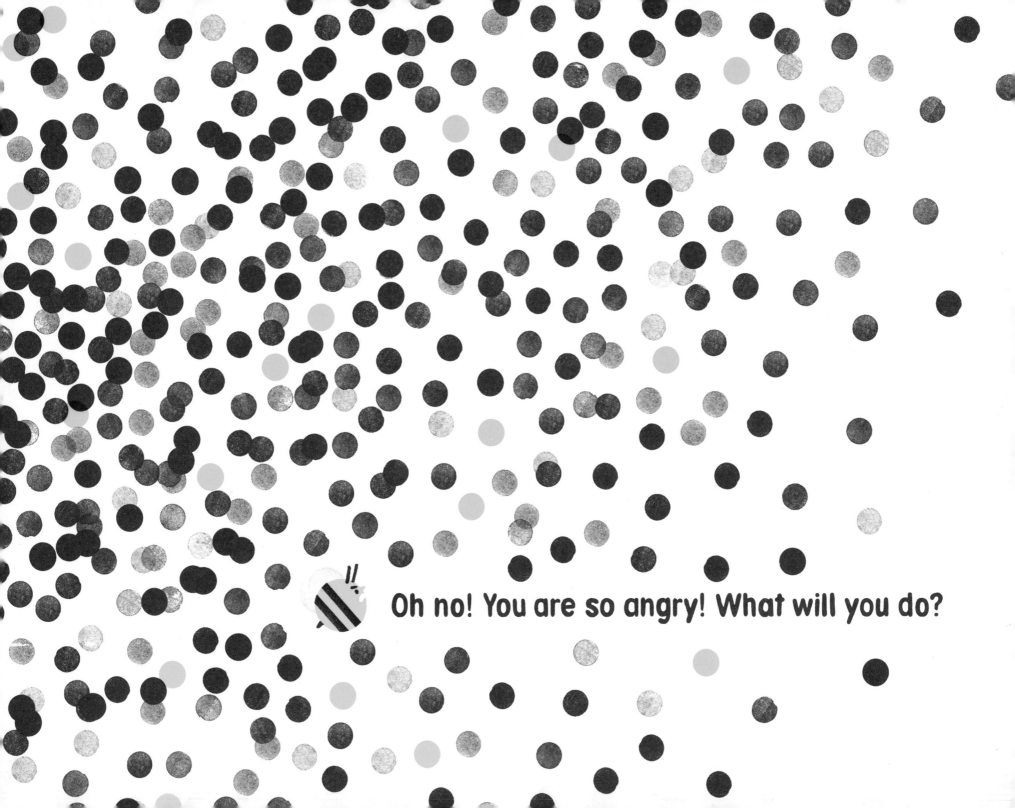

Oh no! You are so angry! What will you do?

Swarm of bees! Swarm of bees!
Will you sting the sailor?

No! He's been on a ship for nine months and is hurrying to hug his mother.

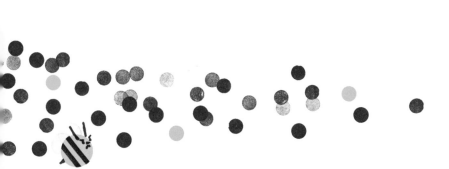

Swarm of bees! Swarm of bees!
Will you sting the mother?

No! She's about to tell the bricklayer all about her new hairdo.

Swarm of bees! You are still feeling angry!
But you can't sting anyone at the food truck!

The chefs are chopping onions as quick as they can, and the customers are deciding what to drink with their lunch.

You can't sting the cat!

The cat is trying very carefully to hide in the grass.

And, cat, you can't pounce on the bird!

It has a worm in its mouth!

Swarm of bees! Swarm of bees!
You can't sting the man in the second-floor
apartment watching television!

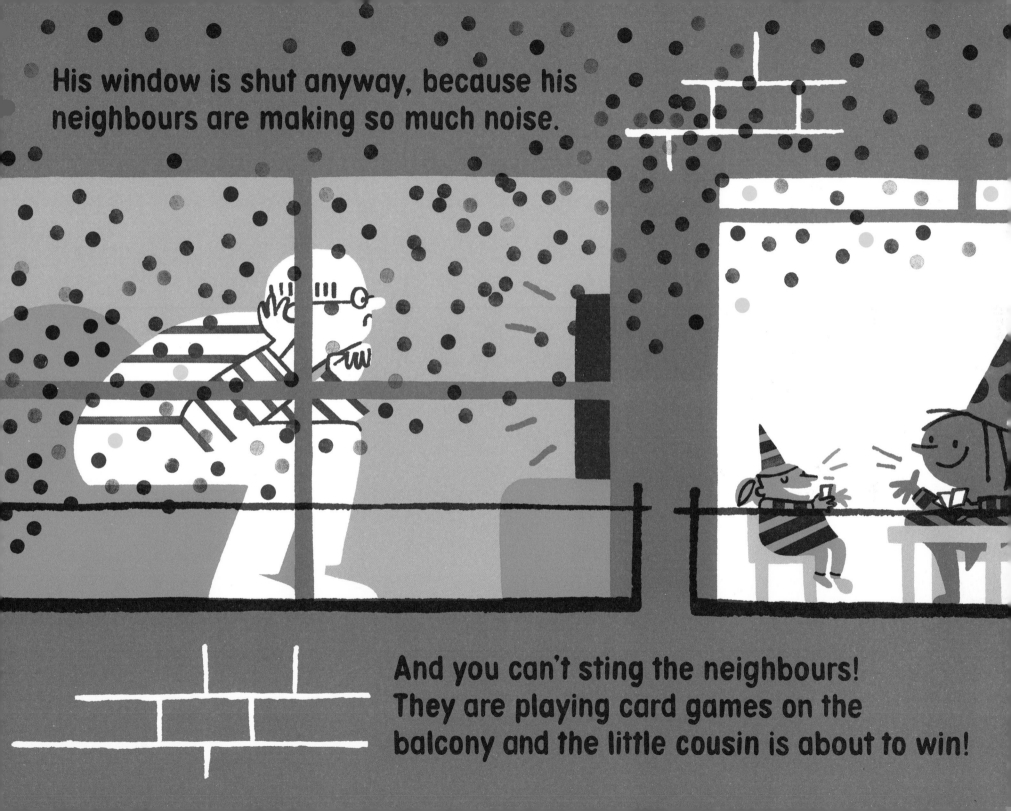

His window is shut anyway, because his neighbours are making so much noise.

And you can't sting the neighbours! They are playing card games on the balcony and the little cousin is about to win!

You are still angry,
but you can't sting the little cousin!

She already hurt herself today when
she stubbed her toe, and that's why
she's wearing that bandage.

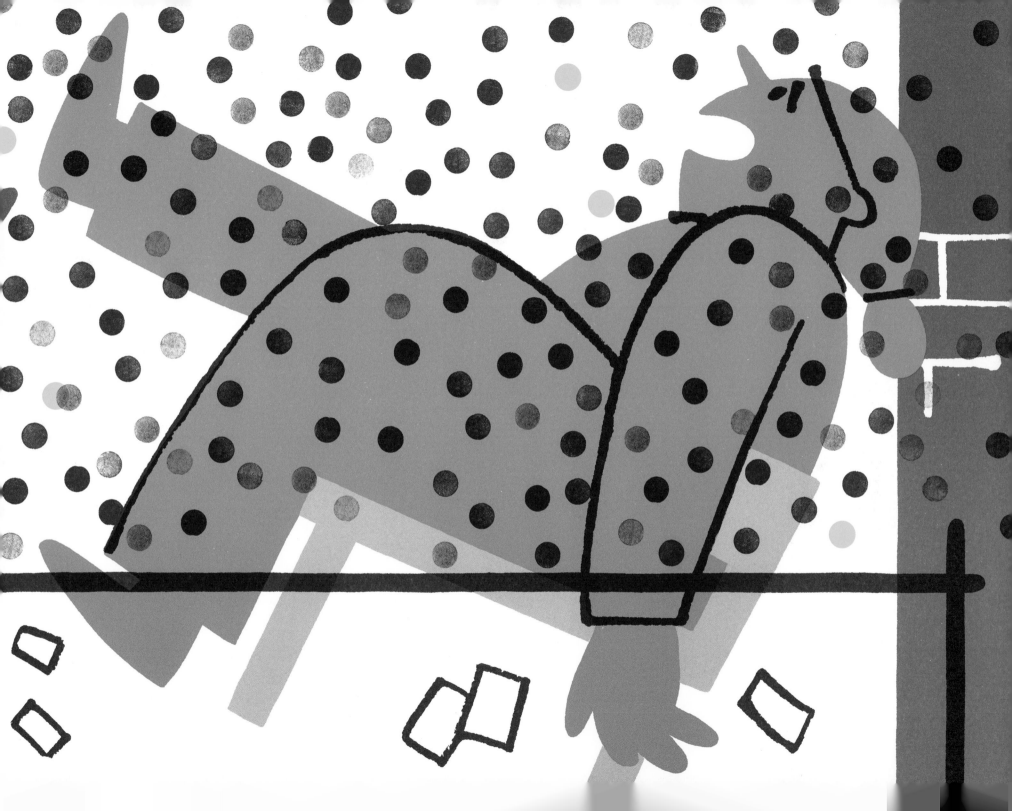

Swarm of bees, are you going to sting the boy? He keeps throwing tomatoes!

He threw one at the little cousin and stained her bandage!

He threw one at the neighbour's window and made a mess!

He threw two tomatoes at the cat

and three tomatoes at the bird,

who dropped the worm into
a tomato on the ground!

The boy threw a bunch of tomatoes at the food truck! He shouldn't do that!

The boy threw tomatoes at the bricklayer, and he threw tomatoes at the mother's hairdo, and look! Swarm of bees!

He threw a tomato at the sailor, and the sailor is chasing him!

Where did they go, swarm of bees?
Where is everybody?

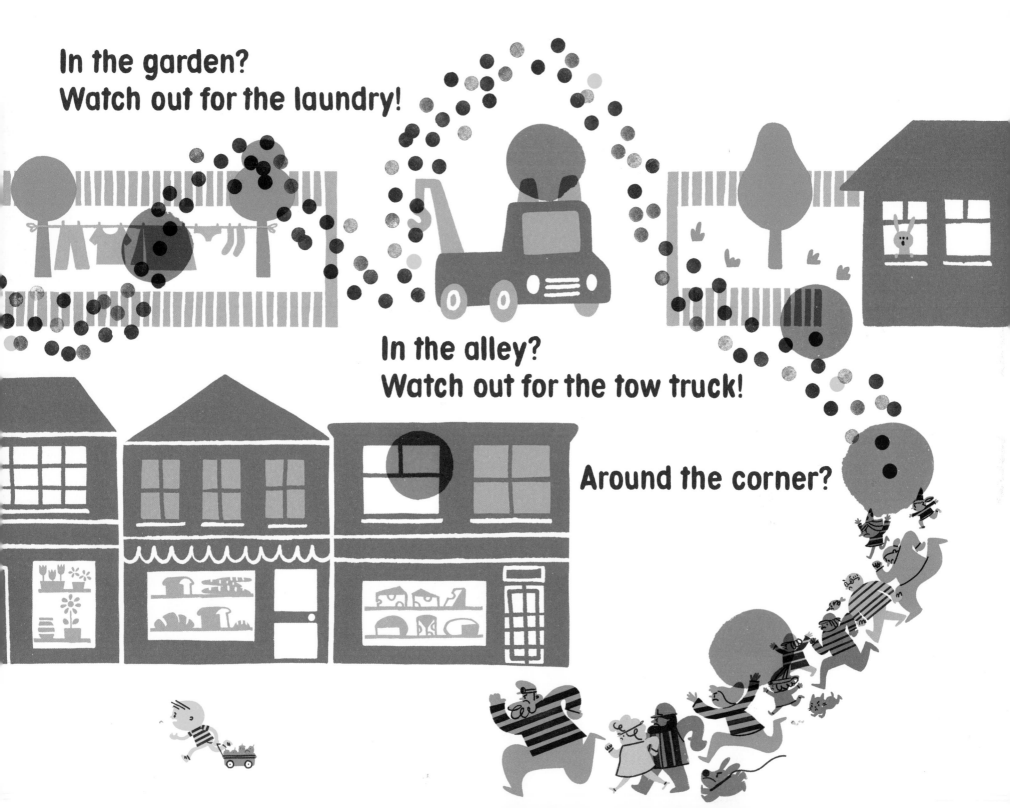

In the garden?
Watch out for the laundry!

In the alley?
Watch out for the tow truck!

Around the corner?

Watch out for the beekeeper!

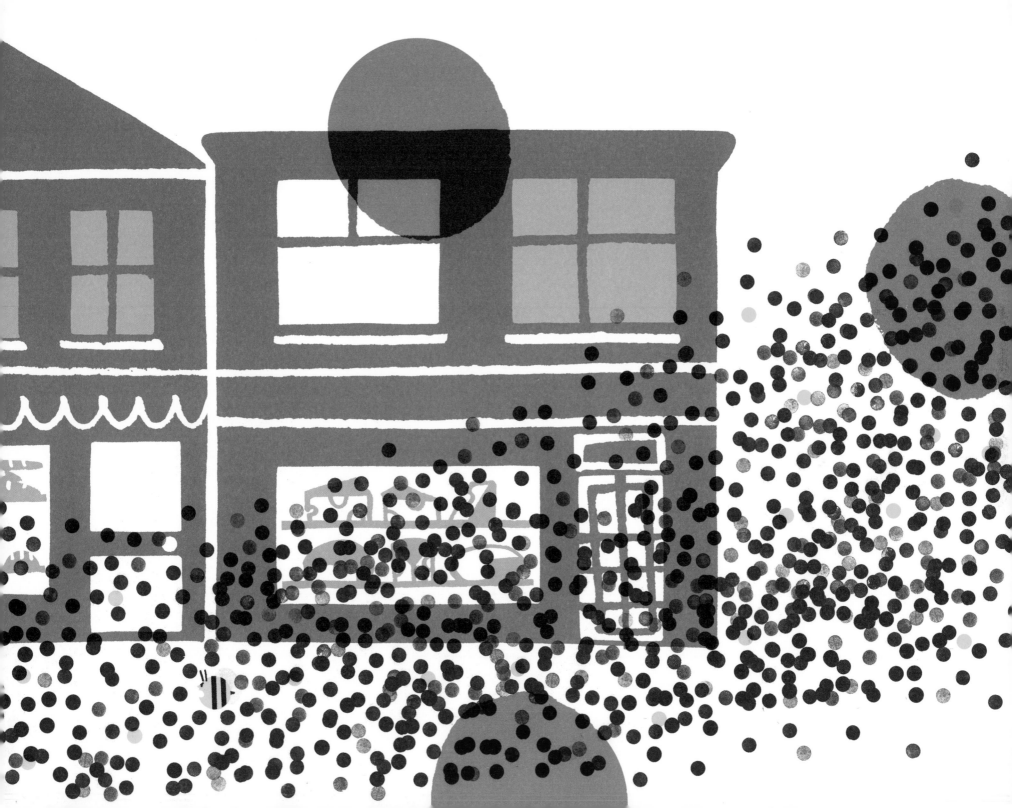

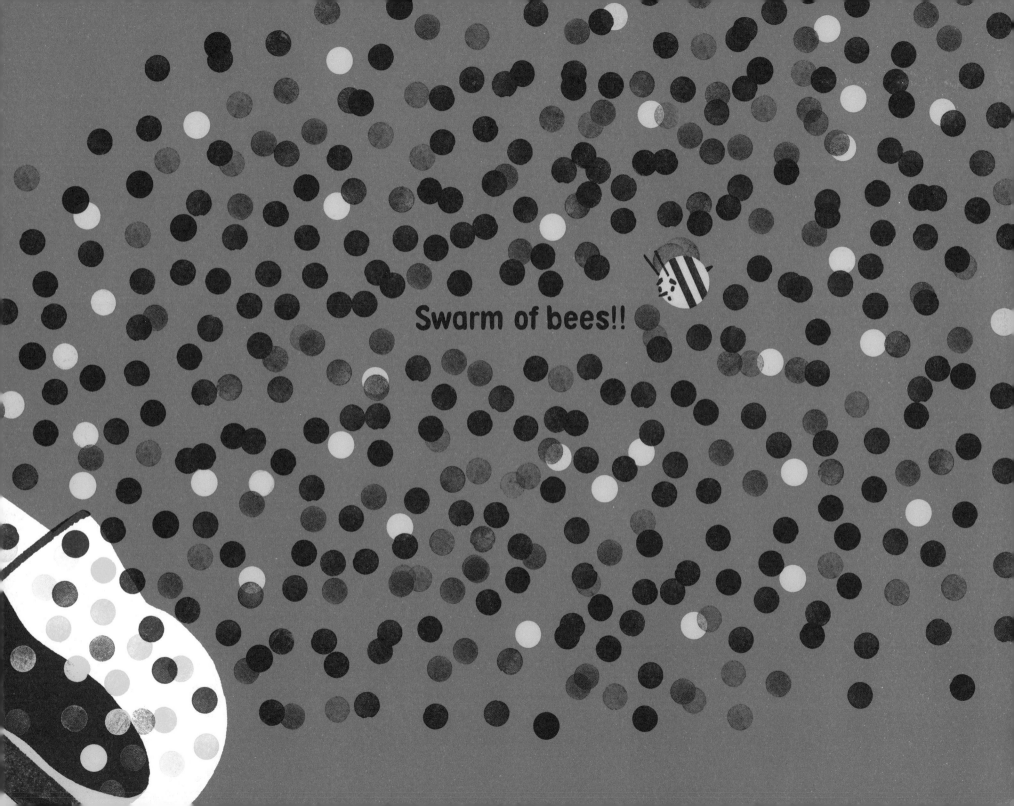

Swarm of bees!!

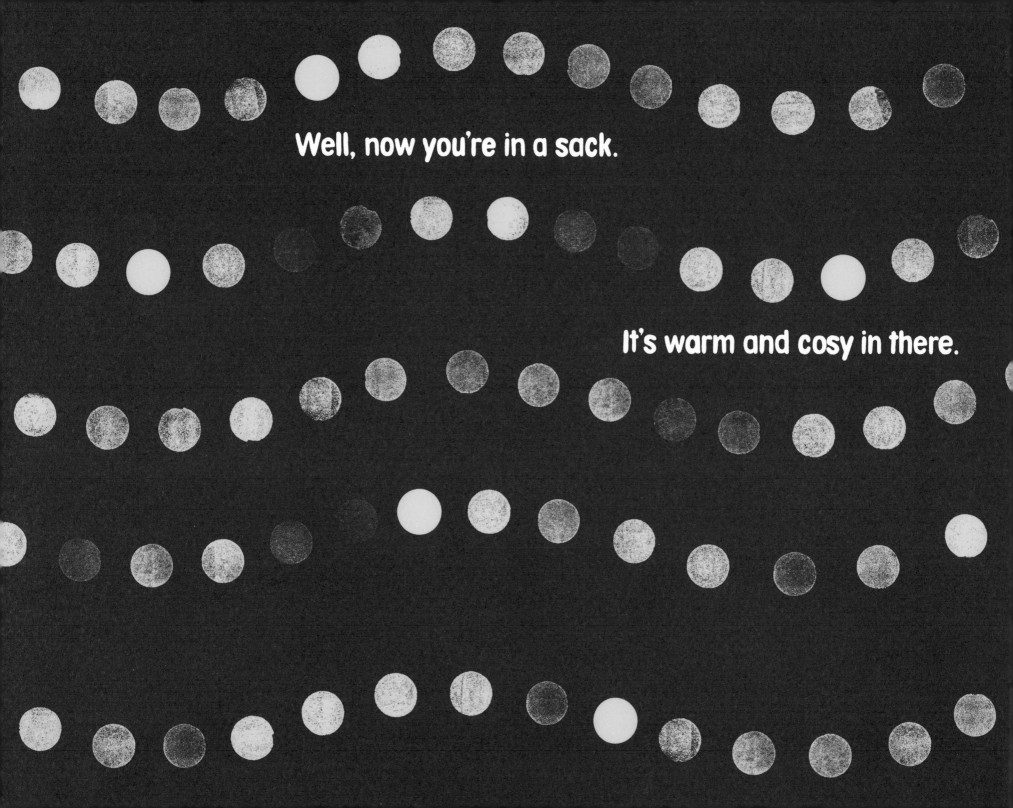

Well, now you're in a sack.

It's warm and cosy in there.

You calmed down

and soon you'll be going home.

It can feel good to be angry.

It can feel better to stop.

And now...

... it's time to clean up all the tomatoes.